By Lynn Hodges & Sue Buchanan

A Song of God's Love

Illustrated By John Bendall-Brunello

Dear God, It's Me!

ZONDERkidz

ZONDERVAN.com/
AUTHORTRACKER
follow your favorite authors

To my parents Mary Jane and Maynard Davis, who taught me early on
that "connecting" with God in prayer is so very simple. And to my girls,
Dana and Mindy, I dedicate this book as a reminder of THAT truth.
—Sue Buchanan

For my nephew Charlie his wife, Janet and their three children,
Oscar, Joe, and Theo because they all love elephants!
And, as ever to my wonderful wife, Tiziana.
—J.B.B.

Dear God, It's Me!
Copyright © 2005 by Lynn Hodges and Sue Buchanan
Illustrations © 2005 by John Bendall-Brunello

Requests for information should be addressed to:
Zonderkidz, Grand Rapids, Michigan 49530

Library of Congress Cataloging-in-Publication Data

Hodges, Lynn.
    Dear God, it's me : a song of God's love / by Lynn Hodges and Sue Buchanan
; illustrated by John Bendall Brunello.— 1st ed.
        p. cm.
    Summary: Expresses the knowledge that God will be near anyone who calls
upon him, from the time they throw off the covers in the morning until it is dark
again, through illustrations, song lyrics, and an accompanying music CD.
    ISBN 978-0-310-70645-8 (hardcover)
    1. Children's songs. [1. God—Songs and music. 2. Songs.] I. Buchanan, Sue. II.
Bendall-Brunello, John, ill. III. Title.
PZ8.3.H6655De 2005
782.42—dc22

                                              2004005899

Editor: Barbara J. Scott
Art direction and design: Jody Langley

Printed in China

08 09 10 11 12 • 9 8 7 6 5

The LORD is near
to all who call on him.
—Psalm 145:18a (NIV)

Before you throw back the covers
and your feet touch the floor,

ask God to show you what he has in store

for the day that's just starting, from beginning to end,
God says he'll be near you if you call on him.

Dear God, I am calling...please listen...it's me!
You know all about my day from a to z!

You know when I'm frightened, sad or alone.
Please stay close beside me. Make my heart your own.

He wants to be near you
all day long while you play.

He cares what you think,
and he cares what you say.

Yes, he cares where you're headed...
knows your outs and ins.

God says he'll be near you if you call on him.

Dear God, I am calling...please listen...it's me!
You know all about my day from a to z!

You know when I'm frightened, sad or alone.
Please stay close beside me. Make my heart your own.

Your world will grow bigger,
and you'll stumble and you'll fall.

Your questions won't be
simple
like they are when you
are small.

You can count on his promise
when life is in a spin.

God says he'll be near you if you call on him.

Remember his promise. Remember his word
at night when it's dark and your prayers have been heard...

through the day that's now over,
fun-filled to the brim.

God says he'll be near you
if you call on him.

Dear God, I am calling...
please listen...it's me!

You know all about my day
from a to z!

You know when I'm frightened, sad or alone.
Please stay close beside me. Make my heart your own.

Please stay close beside me.
Make my heart your own.
Thank you, God. Amen.